THE

WILD

FRONTIER

By

K.M. Rice

For Grammie,
whose love of the West continues to roam in the
wilderness of our hearts, even after she is gone.

Prologue

She was confused, like all of us, when he died. Fortunately for me, I'd faced death before and I remembered more about the motions of loss and the feelings of guilt. Lord knows, that don't make it any easier to bear.

He died in battle, like we all knew he'd want, but it was still such a waste. The first few weeks after a death like that are always trying. You question things you didn't use to think twice about. You stop noticing colors.

Lark took it pretty hard at first. I was worried about her. She had dark circles under her eyes and I never saw her eat. I'd try and talk to her but she'd go and push me away. But after some time, there was a change and she began to smile again. Every once in a while I'd catch her with a wistful look on her face. Trailing her fingers over grass, staring up at the canopy of leaves, cocking her head at a fire, or gazing at mountains. Just gazing, as if she was waiting for something.

I'll admit it, I was pretty confused. But she seemed like she was moving on. She seemed to find her balance again, so I let it alone. Best not to start trouble where there is none.

And she's no pushover, my sister. We'd grown up on the borderlands, orphans when I was ten and she was seven — the children of indentured servants. The pox that took our parents near took Lark, as well, but she licked the fever. We were taken in by the German neighbors over the hill, Fuhrmann, but they already had six children and even more spoons to beat us with. At the bottom of the pecking order, we learned to earn our keep. How to cure tobacco and snare rabbits. Lark was always right there beside me, working in the fields and checking the traps, just as good as me, or any boy for that matter. She loved it, too. So much more than the cooking and corsets Mrs. Fuhrmann tried to force on her. As if she was one of her daughters allowed to sleep in the bed. As if she didn't stand out with her brown hair amidst all those blondes. As if she didn't prefer to run with the boys and wear trousers.

Now, don't get me wrong. The girl used to try to nurse ailing rodents and birds back to health and held funerals when they didn't make it. She loved those funny-faced paper dolls that you could dress up. She got hair ripped out once for trying on our foster mother's wedding dress without asking. There ain't nothing unladylike about my sister except her clothing, and that's only because we always lived miles from town. Miles. Maybe more.

You see, when you grow up outside of buildings and on deerpaths instead of streets, you aren't properly educated. A body doesn't know what or who to hate. You remember that now.

The thing about opportunities is that they're worthless if you don't have the gumption to take them. If there was one thing the pair of us knew growing up sleeping in the dirt by the fire after fighting with a stranger's children all day, was that we needed to get away. Far away. We dreamed of the West, so when I was twenty-four and had finally saved enough to fund the endeavor, my little sister was once more at my side. Traveling with just the two of us, it was too dangerous to cross through Indian Territory, so we waited until we'd formed a small party, consisting of Lark, myself, and two middle-aged brothers: Frank and Steven Smith. They were blacksmiths by trade who'd heard tell of the Spaniards in the Mexican territories getting their horses shod with gold shoes. They figured a place like that would have room for men like them. Never mind that gold is a terribly soft metal to be used for shoeing anybody. Lark, on the other hand, thought they were pompous and slow, like crawdads on land, on account of their lack of knowing things like how to fell a tree or raise a tadpole into a frog.

We started out after the first snow melt. That's where we met him.

Not long after crossing the Ohio River, he came out of the shadows one night, asking to share our fire. By the looks of him I could tell he was part Indian, but he had these piercing green eyes that would make any man trust him, and by the state of his clothing and gear, he'd seen better days. We later learned that he was part Crow and had been a captive of the Sioux for many years before he'd been traded to a white fort as a slave. He had the scars to show for it. So he joined up with us, heading West as our scout, since all his family were dead anyway and as a half-breed, he didn't have much where else to go. We Scottish can understand that.

He went by the name of Charles, though I couldn't think of anything more ill-fitting. He didn't look like a Charles. He didn't act like a Charles. Hell, he wasn't even a Christian. He was a lost brave, a head taller than me and powerfully built, yet quiet as a stream. And not in a peaceful, noble savage sort of way. In a wounded way. Like he was broken. Like he was only ever half-there. Normally he wouldn't speak unless spoken to, though from what she's told me of their story, Lark seemed to tease both life and smiles out of him. He wore his hair in a ponytail with no coup feathers. He donned the leather breeches of his people and the linen shirt of a white man. He seemed torn between two worlds. I don't know which one's heaven he eventually went to. I just hope he's all right.

One day, months after he died, I caught Lark with that wistful look, watching a spider build its web. I asked her what she was doing.

"Just listening."

I listened, too, but I couldn't hear anything. "To...?"

She gave me a funny look, like she was a priest and I'd just asked what a church was while standing in one. "A song, Jasper. A song in the leaves."

5

Lark turned away from me without further explanation and I knew I just didn't understand.

I think now I know what it was she heard that day, but I'll never be sure. Only she'll know, because I've never asked. And I can't tell you the end of this story, either, because I don't know how it ends. Maybe I never will.

But you know what? That's just fine by me. It adds to their greatness in my mind — to their quiet legend. It keeps the mystery and the story alive, and we all can wonder together. And it will just keep on going, like the wind. As it should.

I.

It was the way Charles would only come to the fire to eat then would return to the edge of the light every night that made Lark think of the tall, broad-shouldered man as a sentry more than a part of their motley group. He had a face that she could have considered fair if not for the way his expression rarely changed. After a month or so of travelling together, she knew all she wanted to know about the blacksmith brothers, Frank and Steven, and even more that she didn't want to know. Charles, however, had only been with them for a week, and in that time the most he'd ever said to Lark was "Pleasure" when they first met. Sometimes she would glance his way and find him averting his gaze to the ground, as if he'd been observing her. Whether like a vulture or a curious raccoon, she couldn't tell.

She didn't have space in her thoughts at first to pay him much heed since she was sleeping under the trees and riding so much every day that her backside had never hurt more. Moving. Every morning was a new trail shimmering with dew. A new pine grove or meadow. A new frontier. And crossing through it all excited her more than anything ever had in her life.

"A trout supper," Jasper announced as the group followed a deerpath through the trees, their horses taking stray bites at shrubs as they passed. The dappled mule that carried the majority of their supplies was tethered to his saddle and followed closely behind. "That's what I'm hankering for. Fried up in a little bit of bacon grease."

Frank and Steven groaned, as if they didn't have paunches to live off of. "With a side of mustard."

"Mustard?" Jasper scoffed. "Now why the hell would you go ruining a perfect dish like that with mustard?"

"It's not perfect until it *has* mustard," Frank insisted.

Jasper spurred his mount to better lambast the blacksmith and the mule started to trot after him only to slow once the end of his tether slipped onto the ground. Knowing there was no use in trying to pull her brother out of a heated discussion, Lark prodded her mare towards the pack animal, intending to grab his lead, only to have the mule try to bolt into an ash grove, headed for the lush green grass of a clearing.

Before she could shout to her brother or the others, Charles trotted his gelding, weaving through the trunks and heading off the mule before it could make it out of the grove. Though the others noticed the clanking of their tinware on the animal's back, they didn't slow their pace.

Charles herded the dappled mule until it gave up on its attempted escape. Leaning down, he gathered up the rope and led the mule back to Lark. He handed her the end of the lead with a furtive, owlish glance at her face.

"Thank you, Charles," she said as she tied the rope to her pommel.

The only acknowledgement that he'd heard her was the fact that Charles held her gaze for a heartbeat longer than usual before staring at his mount's mane. Sometimes she forgot that he even knew English.

While Jasper and the blacksmiths continued to argue, Lark rode in silence beside the scout. One of her foster brothers had been quiet, as well, and as such it was always easy to forget the boy was there. The opposite was true with Charles. His presence was like a bright color, or the warm winds in the coming of a storm. Full of potential and the unknown.

"You're welcome, Miss Ferguson," a low, hoarse voice said.

She stared at him in pleasant surprise. He may have been five minutes late in a reply but it was a reply. And from that day on, he held his gelding back so that he could ride beside her whenever Jasper was in the lead. On the ground, Charles kept his distance, scouting the perimeter of their camps, gazing at the horizon, but always with Lark the nearest of all of them. Like he was a compass needle and she was his pin. As if it was the first time he'd ever ⟨...⟩ if he knew that she liked to care for wounded ⟨...⟩ as if he wanted to say more than "you're welcome" but never did.

If the others noticed the subtle shift in the gravity of their group, they didn't remark on the change. Lark didn't mind. Mr. Fuhrmann, her foster father, refused to trade so she had never seen an Indian up close before. Much less one with flecks of copper in his scant stubble and with jade eyes. And she'd never seen a person hold so still. He would often take watch at the edge of the trail, the tall grass or ferns swaying around his solid figure in the breeze, as if he wasn't a man at all. One such night as she sat by the fire, the silver light of the moon hugged the side of Charles' body and highlighted the curves of his face as he returned her gaze from afar. His eyes were hooded in the shadows but the wide arch of his cheekbone and the corner of his full lips were illuminated, reminding her of granite. It was the first time she realized how much she would miss him if he ever rode with someone else.

"Lark," Jasper hissed, yanking her attention back to those in the orange glow of the fire, "what did you see? A wolf?"

"We're close now," she softly replied, her gaze still on the sentry, even as he turned his back on the group.

"Close to what?"

"The mountains."

"They'll be hell to cross," Steven remarked with a sigh, shaking his head, his thick mustache catching the firelight and making it seem to move on its own.

The mountains. The following morning, after watering their horses, Lark spotted Charles standing watch over the mountains like a lithic guardian. Stepping up to his side, she gazed upon the snow-covered ridges that rose like hoary shrines. Their chiseled gray and stained crags made her blood rush through her chest like an invigorating waterfall and she couldn't look away. The sensation was intoxicating and strange, for the mountains were tall enough to have grown bald and Lark never liked being very far from trees. But maybe it was the promise of a place so rugged that even pines couldn't grow that so excited her.

The other men argued over which pass to take and while Lark knew that Charles ought to offer an opinion, her shoulder-companion was silent. His expression was placid in the dawnlight as he faced west and Lark wondered if he'd even noticed her approach.

Jays sounded an alarm in the forest behind them and some of the docility slid off of the scout's face. When he flicked his eyes to hers, they were tight and his hand slid to rest on the hilt of his knife, making her tense.

"I don't rightly care if there are still storms in the hills," Jasper was hissing at the blacksmiths. "I'd rather face a blizzard here than in the Rockies."

"You're so damn worried about being waylaid that you aren't even thinking about the practicalities of —"

"The point is, we ain't all in accord," Steven offered in a placating tone.

Bridles jingled and Charles was now standing at his full height, watching the woods as statuesque as the horses whose ears were perked as they stilled and listened to something beyond sight. When the scout rested a feather-light hand on Lark's shoulder blade then stiffly moved to stand in front of her, she knew without a doubt that he'd more than noticed her approach. He'd absorbed her presence.

"What do you suggest, then?" Jasper replied, exasperated. "A vote?"

"Amongst us three," Frank added.

"What, Charles and my sister have no voice?"

Lark's skin crackled and flushed at that and she parted her lips to comment that they weren't just a woman and an Indian out here when suddenly she was shoved to the ground by a large hand. Charles hopped over her and withdrew his knife, dashing into the midst of the other men just as musket shot cracked so loudly that it ended their argument. The lead thudded into a tree behind the five, splintering off flaking bark. Before any of their party could even move to fetch their own firearms from their saddles, a man in a red cap and furs stalked out from behind the brush. One musket was slung over his shoulder while another was aimed at the group. He led a dog who was burdened with packs and shouted at them in French, his cheeks ruddy below a dark, greying beard, his blue eyes wide and manic like the blizzards the blacksmiths feared.

Rising to her knees, Lark was careful to move slowly, the crack of the gunfire still ringing in her brain. The man jerked the barrel of his weapon upwards as he repeated his command, and the men reluctantly held out their hands in surrender as the musket leveled on Jasper.

"*Couteaux*," the man repeated. "*Couteaux!*" He jerked his head at their waists and Charles was the first to toss his knife onto the ground. With a sigh, Jasper followed suit, then the brothers.

Lark leaned back on her hip, hiding her own blade. Though the Frenchman's gaze lit upon her at her motion, he didn't give any sign that he thought she was armed. Instead, he side-stepped towards their horses and supplies, tugging his dog along with him. When Lark realized that he'd singled out her brother as the main target, she wished she was a man or a horse who could pommel the whiskers right off his leathery skin and the light right out of his eyes. Her palm pressed against the dead leaves and the hilt of her knife. She'd never been very good at throwing but was willing to try.

"Boys," Frank said softly as the Frenchman glanced over their saddlebags, "I reckon he intends to rob us."

"*Une femme?*" the intruder asked, jerking his head at Lark before lowly chuckling as he continued to shuffle towards her.

No one needed to speak French to understand why his focus had been diverted from their goods. The heat thrumming through Lark's veins cooled as the man's blizzard eyes warmed and drank her in, as if inspecting a kill he was butchering. The hairs that rose on her arms and back told her that she was an animal and that animals fought. Animals gnashed at throats. But as much as she wanted to chomp on his windpipe, she couldn't move.

"*Une juene femme.*"

15

"I ain't no nothing *femme*," she whispered.

The Frenchman flicked his fingers at her, beckoning her to rise. Like a parent collecting a child from a playdate. His musket and gaze was still leveled on her brother's torso. As if to emphasize her situation, the bearded man wiggled his trigger finger.

"*Viens avec moi.*"

"Lark," Jasper began lowly, "don't you move a muscle. I'll —"

The Frenchman jerked his head with another command then glanced Lark's way to gauge her reaction. In his momentary lapse of focus, Charles strode forward. The intruder immediately swung his musket to aim at the scout but the large man didn't slow and his stride looked more like someone who had run out of patience than a man facing down the barrel of a gun.

"Charles," Jasper hissed at the same time the Frenchman started shouting.

Lark curled her feet under her as Charles's long-egged gait closed the gap between him and the bearded man. She tensed, expecting the sulfur of another shot to burn her nose, but instead of firing, the mountain man hauled his musket back and swung. The scout threw up his left forearm to parry the blow and the wood and metal thudded against his skin with a thump like a falling rock. Stomping on the other man's moccasined toes with his heeled boot, Charles punched the Frenchman in the face which sent his pack dog into a barking fit. The maneuver happened so quickly that Lark lost herself in the swiftness of it all and didn't remember ever unsheathing her knife. It was just suddenly in her hand and she was standing and shaking but too afraid to stick the metal into a man.

The gun landed in the leaves with a dull thud. The Frenchman swung back at the scout with a curse but Charles' elbows were raised around his head like a shield and the smaller man couldn't get in a decent blow. When he tried again and once more failed, Lark realized that the only time she'd ever seen a man defend himself in the way Charles did was when they'd passed by a boxing match while waiting for the Smith brothers in town.

The intruder tried for a third hit but while his arm was arching back, Charles's fist connected with his jaw. The Frenchman staggered and fell to one knee beside his yapping dog. Charles kicked the fallen musket away then let out a howl, curling in on his own fist as Frank lunged for the weapon.

The other men recovered their blades while their scout whined and shook out his hand, gritting his teeth and stomping in frustration. The Frenchman was still stunned and kept trying to stand only to slip back onto the ground, as if he was a drunkard staggering up a slope, and the animal in Lark caught scent of his weakness. She darted forward and kicked him in the gut as hard as she could. The toe of her boot felt dull against the man's belly and she wanted it to feel sharp, so she kicked again. He coughed and whined, yelping in his own tongue.

Then an arm was around her and yanking her backwards so swiftly that she nearly lost her balance. When she jerked her head to the side to see that it was Jasper, she realized that she'd raised her knife and was poised to strike him. Deadlier than a rattler, for she had no awareness of even raising her arm.

Finally on his feet, the Frenchman gathered up his dog's leash and stumbled back to the trees, trying to curse them around the displacement of his jaw. The blacksmiths harried and hounded him as if they were chasing off a coyote, pelting him with rocks.

"Lark?" Jasper whispered and she dropped her knife. "We weren't gonna let him touch you."

"I know."

Her brother's arms eased around her, and once he was sure that she was herself again, he let her go. Lark brushed some of the stray wisps of hair out of her face and picked up her knife. The pack dog chirped out a whine as it was struck by a rock in the shrubs but she didn't turn around to look. Charles was off to the side, watching her as if he could read her every breath, his right hand curled in to his chest. Against the dark leaves of the trees still in shadow she could see that he was steaming. Which reminded her that it was still quite cold, and quite early in the day.

"All right then," Jasper announced as the blacksmiths returned to the camp. "Let's get the hell out of here."

Even the Smiths weren't in a mood to argue, and as the company collected their mounts, Lark caught Charles stiffly uncurling his fingers, testing his damaged knuckles.

No one much spoke of the incident all day, as if to bring it up again would curse the quiet of the woods that surrounded them as they rode nearer to the mountains. They made camp in the foothills and Frank fixed up some supper.

"Yep," Jasper sighed satisfactorily after eating. "Sure is nice to have a woman's cooking."

Frank thanked him cordially then turned his attention to their scout who was once again at the edge of camp, watching the climbing moon shift the shadows on the crags above. An owl hooted from nearby, followed by an answering call from another in the distance, and Lark couldn't tell if it was the bird conversation Charles was listening to or if he could hear the voices of the mountains.

"Come on over and sit a spell, Charlie," Jasper called.

When the scout didn't react, the other men exchanged amused expressions. Only Lark saw Charles' shoulders rise and fall like a tree limb in the breeze as he softly sighed.

"Ain't he the damnedest thing?" Frank chuckled. "How the hell could a boy like him learn to fight like that?"

"Soldiers and Sioux get bored," Charles replied, and his deep voice cut through their amusement. Twisting his torso to face them, he arched a brow as the nearby owl hooted again. "And I learn quickly."

"Were you a prize fighter?" Jasper asked.

Charles eyed the flames and Lark was certain she saw him glance at the other men's' weapons before he made his way over to the ring of yellow light. He paused beside Lark and held his good hand out near the heat. "When I didn't win, I got the cat."

"They whipped you for that?" Steven asked. "That don't make any sense. Downright counterintuitive if you ask me."

"Motivation," was Charles' only answer. He turned his injured hand over and inspected the swelling in his fingers. "Of course, back then, my knuckles had rags for protection."

The Smith brothers gazed at him for some time, their eyes glistening in the firelight as if they were trying to decide if he was lying or telling the truth.

21

"Well, I for one sure am appreciative," Jasper said, stretching his legs out before him and crossing them at the ankles. "I'm sure we would've found some way out of that tight spot but..." He shook his head and let out a low whistle. "I ain't ever seen a man face down a musket like that."

"How'd you know he wouldn't shoot?" Frank asked.

Charles crouched, his eyes distant. When he spoke, it was to the fire, and Lark was glad he didn't look at her or he might notice her admiring his courage.

"When I was a captive of the Brulé," Charles began, speaking slowly, "I learned many things. One of them was how to stop gunfire from igniting."

The blacksmiths leaned forward a bit more while Jasper lowered his brows.

Charles chanced a glance at Lark, as if they shared some secret, and she smiled without knowing why.

"How the hell does a body learn that?" Jasper asked breathlessly.

"It takes time," Charles replied, fixing him with a steady gaze. "And skill."

22

Jasper nodded.

"And it helps to notice that his gun wasn't cocked."

Frank blinked, narrowing his eyes. Then Lark snorted, followed by Steven. Jasper sounded pained as he started laughing and when Charles chuckled lowly beside her, she felt the sound warm on her skin and soothe the hairs that had been raised by the Frenchman.

II.

One afternoon, the group came across a lone cabin nestled in a meadow fringed by firs in the foothills. The family invited them all to share a meal, yet once they caught sight of Charles' skin they refused to allow him into their home. Charles quietly accepted and offered to ride ahead to survey the land they'd have to cover the next day.

Lark stood on the cabin porch, watching him ride off with the growing sensation of being caught in a snare. The wife inside the cabin laughed loudly at one of Frank's jokes and Lark looked over her shoulder and into the house. The blonde woman's back was stiff from a corset as she stoked the fire. Her accent was Germanic. Frank, Steven and her brother Jasper took their seats while a toddler squealed as he ran from new person to new person. The husband waved Lark in, stepping towards her. The whole scene was too much like the dirt floor they had slept on as unwelcome children. Lark immediately backed away from him and locked eyes with Jasper through the open door.

"I'm going with Charles."

She hastily mounted her resting mare and loped across the young grass, heading for the trees before the surprised faces of her company and their hosts had the chance to singe her mind. She found the scout about a mile away grazing his horse, just as thunder groaned overhead and rain began to fall. His shoulders were tense as she trotted into the clearing, his cheeks flushed. Though his entire body sagged in relief when he recognized her, Lark noticed the knife he'd drawn at the sound of her mare's hoofbeats.

"I never took too kindly to blondes," she offered by means of explanation and was rewarded with a tired smirk as Charles glanced over her messy brown braid.

"You shouldn't be out here. It's bound to rain," he said, as if the falling water hadn't already thickened into a downpour.

Lark laughed, even when her mare spooked from the bass drum of thunder in the sky. The two sought shelter in a nearby cave that had been carved by the river that once flowed through it and built a small fire. Lark knew a young woman and a young man should never cohabit such a space. At least, she thought she knew. Her foster sisters had been drilled on propriety that had never even been mentioned to her. Like Jasper, she'd learned most of the rules of society by eavesdropping which, she figured, was about all such ideas were good for. Dropping from eaves.

The rain had now let up to a mist, white in the flickering firelight against the dark night sky. The dripping rainwater from the pines made loud *snaps* as it splattered onto dead leaves and living branches. The thick scent of wet earth and plant life filled Lark's nostrils as she breathed deep, drinking in the relative quiet. The popping and soothing hisses of the fire lulled her, it's heat welcome against her shins as she rested with her back and head against a wall of the cave. Charles was seated across the fire from her, bare-chested, arms wrapped around his thighs for warmth. His linen shirt was on his legs facing the flames, drying, his damp tresses undone and fanning across his back.

It wasn't terribly cold. She even had her woolen jacket unbuttoned, but the man shivering across from her had been showing signs of illness all day. He'd been more sluggish than usual, sitting down whenever they dismounted and closing his eyes when he thought no one was looking. His hand had healed from punching the

Frenchman, but now something else was ailing the scout. He shifted, moving his shirt to expose a wetter area, his gaze searching out the night-veiled alluvial plain where their horses grazed. Charles sighed almost inaudibly then rested his cheek against his knees.

Lark felt a smile tug at her lips and started to shrug off her coat. "You're welcome to borrow this, if you —"

"I ain't cold."

The firelight flickered off of his skin and she could see goose bumps. She arched a brow and nestled her coat back on her shoulders. "Of course. How foolish of me."

She smiled to let him know it was a jest. He didn't return the smile, but rather inched closer to the fire, leaving her wondering how the Crow joked, if they joked at all. His skin slid over the gentle bumps of his ribs as he moved, several whip scars on his back catching shadows.

The dripping of the trees outside was lessening and Lark knew Jasper and the others would be probably be bedding down on the cabin's floor for the night. She crouched beside the fire and added more wood. Some of it was still wet and steamed and smoldered in the flames. Sighing, she sat back against the cave wall, flicking a few stray wisps of hair out of her face. Her elbows rested on her knees, her wrists crossed as she gazed at the flames. They drew her in with their siren colors, shifting shades of heat. They seemed to dance and the sparks that rose with the smoke gyred and faded into night. It brought her peace.

"What're you thinking about?" Her trance was broken by Charles' voice, slightly hoarse from being so quiet.

She drew in a deep breath, looking at him then at the flames again. "I was just noticing how the flames take on a shape and life of their own."

Charles rested his chin on his knees, gazing into the fire as well. "They do."

She eyed him for a few more heartbeats, hearing the echoing crack of a whip in her mind. "You probably spent many nights alone when you were..."

Grunting, he sniffed a little and she noted that he sounded congested.

Lark hesitated before she spoke again. "You must've been sorely lonesome."

Keen green eyes flicked to hers then to the mouth of the cave once more. "Sometimes, during the day."

"Why not at night?"

"Well, when I'd," he momentarily paused as he gestured to the flames, "be near a fire I was all right."

"There's little in this world that warmth won't cure."

He shrugged a little. "I reckon."

Charles was looking into the flames again and fell silent. She also watched the yellow-licked wood as the ashes on the rim near the entrance fluttered in the breeze. Nights weren't better for her as a child. Nights were when she wept over the scent of her mother's scalp and the softness of her cheek while Jasper breathed in unbroken sleep at her side.

"Though... more than that." Charles inclined his head toward the fire. "Like you said, there is life there, among the flames." He took in a deep breath and slowly exhaled, beginning to show some weariness.

A corner of Lark's mouth curved up, seeking distraction from the bruises the spoons had once left on her shoulders. "What do you see in the flames?"

"Companions in the warmth. A reminder of the sunrise. Of tomorrow."

"I suppose there's always a new day, ain't there?"

"A new day for remembering."

Remembering. Something about the word caused a prick of sourness in her stomach. Lark leaned forward a bit, trying to catch the young man's gaze. "Charles, you're free now." He looked at her as she spoke. "We're traveling to a new land. The future's yours. Sometimes we have to let go of what's happened to us to realize our possibilities."

"I can't let go."

"You can't, or you don't want to?"

"Both. Because they're the same."

She sighed and leaned back against the cave wall again. "What's the same?"

"The past and the present."

"No, Charles, they're quite different."

"Different? Is that why you couldn't stay in that cabin tonight? Because your past and present are so different?"

Lark stiffened and didn't breathe, just like the time she'd encountered a grizzly foraging in an old log yards away and didn't know if it had noticed her yet. When Charles' gaze softened, she knew that this bear had sensed her approach all along. "You weren't welcome," she whispered.

"I never much am." He rested his chin on his knees again. "Not in my village. Not in yours. You are what you have been. It's the way of things."

She parted her lips to call him a homeless fool who didn't know the first thing about her, but the way he shifted, folding his arms over his stomach before leaning against his legs again with a small shiver, stole the heat right out of her chest. "That's why we're heading West, innit? To wipe all this mess off our backs and finally be clean?"

"No."

"So you'd rather be a prisoner in your own memories?"

"No."

"Then why are you scouting for us? The money?"

He poked at the fire with a thin branch. "I said I'd sometimes get lonely during the day because I'd spend a lot of time remembering what once was. My

31

mother. My half-sister. Then I'd look at who and where I was at that moment, and I'd feel alone. They were gone. But every day I lived in the memories. In the past *and* the present." He looked over at her again. "It's who we are, Miss Ferguson. The past is who we are right here, right now. And that ain't a bad thing."

Maybe it was the way the firelight danced in his eyes, or because she knew that she could've spent the night at the cabin when he couldn't, but she believed him. "But I'm not that foundling anymore."

Charles shifted his weight, his boots making a soft scuffing noise. "That may well be, but without memories we're just bones. Bones and blood. It's good to remember."

"My father had a wide face. His hugs sometimes hurt."

"Mine was a trapper with a flaming beard. They found him in a gulch, his leg black from a snakebite."

He hugged his legs and his loosed hair fell over his shoulders as he gazed into the fire. In that little gesture he showed his smallness that he usually hid so well under a stony mask.

"How old were you when you lost your mother?"

"The Sioux came when I was seven. I almost didn't recognize her body or my sister's after the raid."

"Savages," she whispered.

"Men," he softly corrected. "Just men."

Lark had long ago hidden the images of her dying parents from her mind. Such ugliness. Such betrayal of what they looked like in life had no place in her memories. Yet Charles remembered like a ceremony, as if such wretchedness was important to who his family had been. Or maybe it wasn't about his family at all. Maybe it was about accepting the hideous underbelly of violence and betrayal as a part of a person, like a blemish or thick eyelashes. After all, Lark didn't know who she'd be if she'd grown up in town attending church socials.

As the wind picked up again she noticed that Charles started to quiver and he shifted, hunching in on himself even more. His eyes were closed and he was beginning to drift. His pride would be the death of him and so would hers. After all, she couldn't much fathom a life in a dress any more than Charles could hide the hint of red in the handful of hairs on his chin.

A loud slap jerked her out of her thoughts. Charles had started to fall over in his sleep and had flung out a palm to catch himself. She bit her lower lip, stifling a laugh as he looked at her confusedly, momentarily dazed by sleep and fever. She stretched out her legs in front of her and patted her lap. "Come here."

He rubbed his eyes. "I'm fine."

"You've been shaking for the past hour, Charles. You're ill." He looked about to fall asleep again and she snorted at the sight of the large man swaying so precariously. Her noise woke him a bit more.

"You don't have a chaperone," he muttered.

"I can't even spell *chaperone* and besides, I've been alone with boys all my life."

"Not half-breed boys."

"I could have ravaged you ten times by now, so you'd think you'd know that my intentions are pure," she replied with an arched brow as she pulled off her coat.

Charles stared at her, blinking owlishly as his brows twitched together. Then his full lips twisted in a smile as he chuckled and she felt that she had known him for a very long time. After another moment of hesitation, he crawled across the few feet between them and she placed a hand on his temple, guiding his head to rest on her lap. She brushed his hair out of his half-lidded eyes, frowning slightly at how hot his skin was over tense muscles. Never had she felt someone so taut. She draped her coat over his naked torso then rested her chilled hand on his arm, easing her palm down around the hardness of his bicep as if it was a wound. Or as if she'd never before touched a boy.

"Your brother —"

"Hush."

"It's just that I rather like him, and you see, I also enjoy being alive."

"This *is* being alive," she assured as she ran her thumb along the smoothness of his bare skin. He didn't relax from her touch and his tension began to seep into her spine, so she hummed quietly to siphon it out of her back. The hiss and snap of the fire were a lulling accompaniment to her voice.

"Are you singing?" Charles softly asked.

Lark stilled her hand. "I was humming."

"I like it."

"As much as you like my brother?"

"More."

"It's a song my mother used to sing to me."

Charles shifted to grow more comfortable and rested his hand on her knee as she replied. In the span of those few seconds, the oxygen in the cave seemed to thin, and Lark knew that she certainly could spell *chaperone*. Especially when the tense muscle beneath her hand reminded her of just how much damage a bear could cause. How much gentleness tree-shade could provide. How much she enjoyed the deepness of Charles' voice and the scent of his buckskins. Like a saddle. Then the moment cracked and grew when he spoke.

"Won't you sing?"

She hesitated as she tried to forget just how much man she had in her lap. "You want me to?"

Charles sighed, shifting his ear slightly against her thighs. "Your name is Lark."

She moved another lock of his hair, peering down at him, both wanting her brother to turn up looking for her and never wanting to be found again. "Only if you sleep."

He shifted, curling up more against her warmth, muttering some sort of admonishment in his own tongue.

She smirked, tempted to poke fun at his childlike behavior. After humming for a while, she quietly sang.

"Whether near or far away
At the dawn or the close of day,
Whether now or whether then,
You will always have my hand.

Through mountain high and river valley
Through desert sun and winter snow,
Take with you what I give freely,
Yours forever, wherever you go.

Stray not far, stray not far.
Slumber sweetly my shining star
Stray not far, stray not far
You are ever in my heart.

Whether in dream or whether waking
Whether old or whether young
Whether laughing or lost in sorrow,
You will be my only one.

So stray not far, stray not far.
Slumber sweetly my shining star
Stray not far, stray not far
You are ever in my heart."

As she finished the song, the back of her neck flushed. She had always thought of the lullaby as being about the bond between a parent and child, but looking down at the sleeping scout, it struck her that it could just as easily be about anyone cherished. She realized that she'd been running her fingers through his hair as she sang so she stilled her hand, studying her long, pale fingers and stubby, dirty nails. Charles shifted, yet his expression was peaceful and his breathing was even. She traced a line down his bicep. His muscles were soft.

Lark cocked her head as she studied his face, noting the small beads of sweat along his hairline and the smoothness of his skin around his sparse stubble. His height and hardened expressions had always made him seem wizened, as if he was older even than Frank and Steven, yet looking at him now, she saw the hardships lifted, revealing the youth that his grief and time in captivity had stolen from him.

Thinking back to their conversation made her feel older, as well. For nothing could remedy the yellowed pallor and gaping maw of her mother after she'd stopped breathing. Nothing could siphon the blood of Charles' sister back into her body. Nothing could bring motion back to the stiff bodies of the baby rabbits that seized and stiffened in Lark's hands countless times after she had been so sure that they would survive.

But the lullaby of the fire and Charles' steady heartbeat and breathing reminded her that looking under rocks was necessary, as was greeting the writhing, swarming things that thrived in the darkness below. That just because she didn't want a thing to happen didn't change at all the fact that it did. That there was some measure of peace knowing that there were some things in the world no one and nothing could change, even if they hurt. And that hurt wasn't all bad. Pain was temporary and a reminder that she was alive. And that being alive was the most important gift ugliness could give.

III.

By the time they could spot the fort in the distance, Charles' brows had lowered enough to give his eyes a perpetual sneer. Though he had long since recovered from his illness, the scout suddenly seemed feverish. When he halted his gelding at the top of a hill overlooking the realm of the soldiers and looked like he might punch any one of his companions as if they were the French mountain man, the others regrouped.

"We need supplies," Steven insisted. "Beans. Bacon. There aren't many more of these establishments around." The mustached man jerked his head towards the wooden fortress.

Charles' gelding protested as he reined the horse to the side, trying to force it away from the others. The mount snorted and threw his head before dancing in place to tell his human just how much better he knew the world than him. The scout's breathing was labored and as the horse spun in circles, Lark couldn't tell if it was the whites of the animal's eyes or Charles' eyes that she glimpsed.

"I'll stay," Lark announced, walking her mare over to Charles and calming his horse.

Though half his face was hidden in the shadow of his hat, she could tell that her brother was pondering the danger of leaving her in the friction surrounding the fort.

"Those men ain't seen a woman in months," she reminded. "Maybe years. And I ain't exactly inclined to let them leer at me."

"That's a fair point," Steven offered.

"Then here," Jasper added, tugging a rucksack out of his saddlebag. "Take some vittles. I don't know how long we'll be."

He rode the bag over to his sister and lightly shoved her shoulder in farewell before rejoining the blacksmiths. They made plans to rendezvous at several boulders they'd passed that morning. Lark and Charles' horses watched with perked ears as the other three and the spotted mule made their way down the hillside and towards the fort.

"You're not like me," Charles hissed as he continued to pant through his nose. "You don't have to stay here."

"No, I ain't like you," Lark replied, tugging on her reins and walking her horse back towards the rendezvous rocks. "You at least were born with the right parts between your legs."

Her mare swiped at the grass as she walked along and Lark could hear the jingle of his gelding's bridle as he followed. The boulders were nestled in a small clearing on the slope of the mountains they'd been picking their way through, and while the tallest ridges were now at the back of them, a handful of smaller ones still remained. It was slow going and usually chilly, but today the sun was baking the mountainside and making the insects sing as if it was already the middle of summer.

Charles' silence felt like a fly buzzing around her face and crawling on her sweat for the first time. She wanted to snap that her parents had been seen as lower than slaves, and that the English had chased their generation out of the hills and scattered them across distant shores when they cleared the Highlands. That he wasn't the only one whose roots and bowlines had been severed and was now deaf to the voices and tombstones of ancestors whose graves reassured that one belonged to the very soil below. Maybe he could tell that her words were coiling up to bite once they reached the rocks, because he finally spoke and when he did, Lark untwisted inside.

"Steven and Frank, they'll have a merry old time back there. It's Jasper who will be itching to leave. Not from fretting over us, mind you. But from those uniforms." His deep voice was even and he'd stopped panting. "You know why, don't you?"

Lark shook her head as she dismounted.

"Because the only folk who fit comfortably in this world are fools."

Though she tried to force them down, the corners of her lips twisted in a smile. Charles dismounted with a satisfied air about him and the fact that they were once more alone for hours crept down her back like spilled ice water. She busied herself hobbling their horses in the only patch of shade provided by some young cedars then took off their bridles to allow them to graze. Charles tugged on his tunic to air out his chest as he surveyed the slope. She stroked her mare's damp neck beneath her mane as she grazed and Charles shifted to take shelter in the shade, but there was only so long either of them could tolerate the sting of swishing horsetails lashing against their clothing and faces.

Without a word, the scout left, and when Lark watched his meandering form as he kicked over rocks and plucked leaves off shrubs, she realized that she actually didn't mind that her grandmother had lived across the ocean. In fact, the lack of an anchor to her lineage made her feel weightless, like a dandelion tuft that could settle wherever it happened to land.

Once Charles had disappeared behind a grove of pines, Lark cast aside her coat then likewise stripped herself of her blouse, delighted by the sensation of air on her bare arms and shoulders in her camisole and wondered if this was what it felt like for their horses when their sweaty bodies were unsaddled for the day.

"Miss Ferguson?" Charles called.

"I don't rightly know who that is," she hollered back.

"Lark," the scout amended, coming into view in the shade of the pines. "I found water."

After snagging their canteens from their saddles, she made her way towards his voice. Pausing in the shade to catch her breath, she peered about the pines but saw no buckskinned man and no water. A meadow was on the other side of the copse and the grasses there grew tall and thick. Several had tassels and their stalks shone in the sunlight like polished metal but none were wayward. There was no sign that the scout had ever set foot amongst them. Knowing just how close the soldiers were, and just how dark the sun was painting Charles' skin, made the sweat on her neck chill.

"Charles?" she called again.

One of their horses snorted by the rocks and Lark peered over her shoulder, wondering if he'd doubled back to fetch her, but no one was there. A crumb of bark landed on her shoulder and she brushed it off as she returned her attention to the pine needles below her feet that made the ground buoyant and hid all trace of footsteps. Even from the rocks she would have heard the bridles of the soldier's horses had a patrol been sheltering in the grove or nearby. At least, she hoped she would have heard them.

A larger piece of bark landed on her head and as she glared upwards to startle whatever squirrel or chipmunk was dirtying her hair, the canteens clanked together with her surprised jolt.

"Boo."

Charles was several yards above her in a pine, looking far too pleased with himself as he dropped yet another chunk of bark onto her.

"*You*," she gasped, but there wasn't enough air in her lungs or brain to form a proper insult. "You fat ass!"

"Fat?" he spat down with a frown. "From down there only."

She threw the canteens onto the needles. "I'm gonna hit you."

Charles started down, chipping off more bark as he climbed. "A man just can't do no right by you, can he?"

Snatching up a pinecone, she took aim and pelted the scout in the side. Charles let out a startled yelp and she hoped it hurt. Another lay a few feet away and when she grabbed it and spun around to throw it harder, she found Charles hugging the trunk. Instead of timidity, however, he was peering at her as if he was untouchable and knew it. Arching a brow, she took a menacing step forward, only to have the scout giggle. The sound both delighted and infuriated her. He hid his face behind the trunk as she let the second pinecone fly and it harmlessly bounced against the tree, which made his laugh grow.

"You scared me," she tried to bark, but it came out as more of a sulk.

"Why?" he asked, knowing better than to budge, keeping his face hidden on the other side of the pine.

"I couldn't find you."

"I was right here," he replied as he hopped down on the other side of the tree.

"But *I* didn't know that."

Plucking pieces of bark and sap off his palms, Charles stepped out from behind the pine and cocked his head, his eyes reminding her of young leaves haloed by the sun. "I've no intention of going anywhere anytime soon." He jerked his head toward the pinecone on the ground. "Unless, of course, you keep this up."

"You were asking for it."

Charles stepped up to her and she could smell the sap on him and wished it tasted the same way it smelled. He snatched up the canteens, then his fingers brushed over hers, as if it was a moonless night and he didn't trust what he sensed in the darkness. She ought to have noticed his skin on hers right away but instead she only registered it when he pulled his hand away.

"Then let me show you something," he whispered.

She nodded and as she followed him towards the meadow, she bumped the back of his hand with hers and he caught it up, lacing their fingers as he guided her into the sunlight. The grass hissed as they passed through it and the fluttering petals of butterflies drifted amongst wildflowers. There was a streak of darker, lusher green in the center of the glade, marking the path of a spring, and Charles' touch was gentle as he led her to it. The ground sank a little beneath her boots as the soil dampened and while a part of her wanted to tease that water wasn't something to show her, she didn't dare do anything that might make him let go of her hand.

She mimicked Charles as he crouched beside the trickling stream that glinted now and then in the sunlight. When she met his gaze, she hoped that he couldn't see the way each beat of her heart shook her chest, or else he'd know that she thought they could live in this place without ever having to go further west.

"Now," he said huskily, leaning back on his haunches, "close your eyes."

Lark didn't. She couldn't. Not when he was so near and they were so unobserved. When she was so thankful that he'd only been playing a game and that no one had hurt him. Then she remembered that they might still have hours alone and that even if they didn't, they had yet to cross the plains. The other side of the continent was a long ways away and anything and everything could happen in-between. So she closed her eyes.

The stream gurgled and when she felt its cool water on her bare shoulders, her lashes fluttered but she held steadfast and the liquid soon warmed on her skin. Charles dribbled more onto her biceps then slid his palms down her arms, smoothing the water across her skin, painting her with the meadow. She stiffened in unladylike places and wanted him to notice. His hands were at her elbows, guiding her arms out like a tree, then at her waist as he bid her to stand.

"Hold still," he whispered, and she felt the puff of his breath against her neck before the grass hissed as he moved away.

Moments passed and the breeze tickled her skin and her raised hairs, but he did not speak and his presence blended into the glen. Songbirds chirruped and chattered in the pines and the scent of the wet soil reminded her that winter had been cold in this place. That the earth had been around for a long while before she was born and would still be long after she died. That while she walked on two legs she was still an animal and just as much a part of the meadow as the pinks, yellows and blues of the wildflowers. The warm breath of the forest that carried the tang of the drying pine needles touched her cheeks and forehead until she was dissolved into its gusts and could no longer tell where it ended and she began. Nor did she need to.

Charles' voice was soft when it wafted to her across the tassels of the grasses, wrenching her brain away from senses and back into the right angles of words.

"Open your eyes."

She squinted in the return of light as she trickled back into herself. Charles was standing a few yards away and in that moment, she knew what he'd looked like as a little boy.

He read the question on her lips before she had fully formed it in her mind and inclined his head toward her arms. She followed his gaze and a smile blossomed. A butterfly with golden wings and coattails dappled with iridescent blue had alighted on her forearm, drinking from the drying film of water. Another was on her bicep and yet another perched on her thumb, their colors shifting as they pivoted in the sunlight, slowly pumping their wings in place. Her other arm was a similar sight of midnight blue shifting to raspberry then to birch white.

Lark let out a happy puff of air, and when she did, the butterflies took flight, air-dancing with the dozen others that now swarmed, twirling and gliding over the tops of the flowers and the grasses that glistened from the water Charles had painted on them. Their colors twirled against the collage of wildflowers, soaring and swaying in the breeze like the hissing meadow grass.

The scout's gaze was on the trees fringing the glen, as if he could hear the singing of their sighing boughs. Though she knew he was well aware of her approach, he didn't redirect his attention to her until she was a scant foot from him.

"Charles?"

He blinked and held his breath as he turned his face towards hers but kept his eyes downcast as he had when they'd first met. As if he couldn't feel the grass swaying with the steady thud of blood rushing through veins, or maybe because he could feel it all too well. But she couldn't force a man to look at her when he didn't want to, nor was she about to try, so instead, she leaned into him until her cheek was pressed against the dampness of his tunic. Charles supported her weight, and when he placed a hand on the side of her head, he felt like someone trying to stroke a horse he thought might spook.

Lark shifted to peer up at him and his hand fell away, as if he'd already startled her. As he met her gaze there was something tight in his eyes, as if she'd said something to hurt him, when all she wanted to say was that she wished they could share breath.

"Don't look at me like that," she whispered.

"Like what?"

"Like I'm white."

He sighed and she could feel the stream of warmth from his nose against her face. "That ain't it, Lark."

"Then what is?"

The tightness in his eyes grew and for a moment, she fretted that he was harboring a wound she didn't know about. She rested her palms on either side of his chest and pressed them into the warm muscle beneath his tunic. His hand slipped over hers, above his heart, and his fingers curled, as if to pry her away but he couldn't move. The pumping of his pulse under her hand filled her head until she leaned up on her tiptoes to press her lips against his.

"Lark?" Jasper called from a ways off. "Charles?"

Though both blinked with the rush of their surprise and the scout started to lean away, Lark closed the distance between them and planted her mouth against his before releasing him. Charles took a step backwards, as if he'd been shoved, then looked either about to cry or laugh.

"Coming," Lark answered her brother.

Charles shot a nervous glance in the other man's direction, then, once assured that they hadn't been seen, looked back at her lifting a corner of his lips in a funny smile. She gave his arm a light shove as she started towards the pines.

"You were saying?"

The grass hissed as he fell into step behind her. He let his hand bump against her arm as they walked and waited until he was level with her before he replied. When he did, she almost missed a step.

"It's just that some things move beyond words and you think your heart'll break."

IV.

The next time Lark and Charles were alone, they were arranging their bedrolls in the living room of a cabin on the western side of the mountain range. She glanced his way as she unrolled her bedding, the snowstorm wind whistling through some of the planks of the home. The light of the woodstove glowed on her arm and she was grateful that Charles had placed his bedroll alongside the wall, offering her the warmth of the fire. He made a job of arranging his makeshift pillow, keeping his back to her. Now that she had tasted him, there was always the question of when she would do it again. Or when he would.

"I about thought my balls were gonna freeze off."

Both looked over to see Jasper step through the doorway from outside, rubbing his hands together.

"I tell you — don't piss until you absolutely *have* to."

Charles answered first. "Thanks for the advice."

"My pleasure." Jasper warmed his hands by the stove for a few moments. "Frank and Steven are already asleep. They reckon this storm'll have passed through by midday tomorrow. Mr. Fenimore agrees — apparently these winter visitations in late spring ain't uncommon up here. Though if it doesn't clear out he says we're welcome to stay on as needed."

"That's very generous of him." Lark scooted out of the way as Jasper stepped past and wrestled out of his boots, settling into his blankets at the foot of theirs and behind the table in the small room.

The shape of their bearded host popped out from his bedroom. "Are you sure you're not wanting for anything now? I could hang a sheet to create a partition for the lady."

"No, thank you," Lark replied. "We're quite comfortable here, and I ain't seen a lady for some time now."

Mr. Fenimore chuckled. "Figured as much."

Jasper met his gaze from his spot on the floor. "Thank you kindly for the meal."

The bearded man inclined his head. "I'll be retiring now."

The three thanked him and he ducked back into his quarters that he was currently sharing with the blacksmiths.

"When those clouds first rolled in this morning, I sure didn't reckon we'd be bedding down in a fine place like this," Jasper observed.

Lark remained on her haunches by the woodstove, hugging her legs, for crawling into her woolen blanket meant moving closer to Charles. The scout was already lying on his bed, watching the snow appearing out of the dark night as it pelted against the glass of the window across from him. The quiet was filled with the thudding of the flakes and the wailing of the wind. Eerie whistles and howls echoed down the metal pipe of the stove's chimney.

Jasper twisted his torso and arched a brow as he peered at his companions. "You two sure are talkative."

"It's late," she replied.

Her brother groaned then shifted, getting more comfortable. "Only for old maids."

"I'm sure."

When Lark chanced a glance at Charles, she found him watching the other man with a small smile. Jasper's only response was a soft grunt. She pulled off her boots and set them against the wall so that she didn't have to smell them all night then took a seat on her bedroll and undid her braid. The scout's eyes trailed after her fingers as she ran them through her hair in a futile attempt to untangle her tresses. Knowing that he was watching her warmed and tickled her skin. It had been so long since she'd even touched a mirror that she wondered what she looked like. Or rather what Charles saw when he looked at her.

Jasper's breathing grew loud and even, making the scout scoff, "Old maid."

She smiled as she braided her hair, for she had always been envious of the way her brother could so swiftly drop into such a deep sleep. Lying down, she tugged her blankets up to her shoulders and rolled onto her side, studying Charles' profile as he once more focused on the window.

"Do you think we'll do it?" she whispered.

"What?"

"Make it to the coast before winter."

"We're making good time. Near as I can reckon, we'll be all right."

She picked at the strands of brown hair that she'd shed onto her blanket, collecting them like a bird making a nest. "A lot will change once we get there."

Charles lolled his head to the side and she once more felt the warmth of knowing he was thinking about her. Twisting the hair between her fingers into a knot, she basked in his attention before tilting her chin to meet his gaze. His eyes were half-lidded with sleep but traced the lines of her face, making her feel clean and new.

"A lot will change," he agreed, "but not everything."

His focus flitted to Jasper's frame as the other man began to snore. Assured that they wouldn't be overheard, he returned his attention to Lark, and the earnestness of his eyes called to her, pulling her in with the invitation of shelter and deep roots.

"There's one thing that will stay the same."

Though she blinked, she couldn't shift her eyes from his, and she found peace in that unabashed surrender. "What's that?"

Distantly, she noticed that he made no effort to look away, either. Their voices were close to whispers. "It has no end, like the seasons."

Her eyebrows twitched towards each other, her mind sluggish, and she worried her senses were so distracted by him that she wasn't properly hearing his words.

"Like the wind."

"That could mean a lot of things."

"A lot of things, but only one thing."

She waited for him to continue, but when he didn't, she flicked her ball of hair at him. He smirked when it bounced off the bridge of his nose.

"You're not going to tell me, are you?" Lark asked.

Charles busied himself tossing the ball of hair onto Jasper's back then once more met her gaze, pressing his lips together as he shook his head, a smile dancing in his eyes. She'd never been more thankful for the enormity of their journey and the promise of dozens of more moments such as this. Maybe hundreds.

"Then it's a good thing that California is a long ways off yet."

As if in response, Jasper let out a loud snore, causing them both to chuckle. Then Charles rolled over so that his back was to her, tugging his blankets up to his shoulders.

"Don't fret, Lark," he whispered. "You'll know soon enough."

She was the wind, soaring over the granite crags, screaming through the pine needles, speeding faster than any hawk. She was cold and ferocious and free. So very free. And so very wild that nothing could ever come close to her fierce formlessness. Nothing could ever warm her. Nothing could ever love her. Ever. So she screamed. Screamed through the mountaintops. Screamed through the pines. Screamed with the coyotes. Screamed louder than the thunder and rawer than heartbreak.

Lark shot up on her bedroll, flinging the woolen blankets from her with a panicked gasp, glancing wildly about the room, yet the darkness pressed in on her and she couldn't tell if she had a body or if she was still the wind. The pattering against the windowpane and Jasper's heavy breathing were the only reminders of where she was.

She shivered with sweat and jumped when a husky voice asked if she was all right. It took only a moment for her to recognize it as belonging to Charles. She placed a hand over her heart as she closed her eyes, calming. The stovepipe near her screeched in a gust and with relief, she realized the source of her nightmare.

She could feel Charles' sigh of relief against her shoulder and she stiffened, not having thought him so close. But she had a body. She knew that now. The dying embers of the stove aided her adjusting vision and she could faintly see the glow of his white shirt and the glint of metal as he sheathed his knife. He sat back down, giving her space. "Nightmare?"

"I wasn't a person anymore." A small shiver coursed through her as her damp skin quickly cooled in the drafty room.

Charles was quiet, allowing her time to gather her thoughts to speak further.

"It was this damn stove. The gusts in the chimney sounded like... like a howl inside me."

Lark felt foolish admitting to such a childish truth, yet the sentiment quickly absolved when he showed no amusement in her revelation. "We should switch places, then."

"You wouldn't mind?"

He pushed himself up from the bedroll. "'Course not."

Lark rose to move, her braid falling from her back, exposing the bare skin of her neck to the cold and she shivered.

Charles rested his hand on her back as he crouch-walked past then paused, surprise in his voice. "You're trembling."

"It's nothing." She answered too quickly and knew he'd see through her response since her arms quaked with dissipating adrenaline. He slid his hand down her lower back, his other resting on her bicep, making her heart beat faster and a new shiver begin. She was certain now that she had a body. He pulled his hands away and she fought the urge to lean towards him in pursuit. Charles exhaled as he sat back on his haunches, looking from the chilly wall his bedroll was against to the stove. Then he moved and his blankets hit her hand on the floor as he scooted his bedding until it touched hers then grabbed his top blanket, crawling behind her, towards the embers. "I'll sleep here so you don't have to hear the stove. And you won't be cold next to me."

"Thank you."

She tried to keep each action graceful and deliberate so as to not betray how very aware of his nearness she was. Lark matched his calm as he lay down with his back to her, lifting the blanket for her to crawl under behind him. Tugging the wool to her shoulders, she rested her forehead against his back, slightly flush when she felt that his heart was beating as fast as hers. She had a body and so did he. His warmth relaxed her and she focused on breathing evenly to keep up her half of their feigned calm. She couldn't help but notice that he didn't sound very sleepy when he spoke.

"Just remember something happy."

She tilted her head so her chin was nestled beside his spine, curling up her legs, careful not to bump him. Her heart was beginning to slow and she tucked her hands against her breastbone beneath her throat, soothingly warm.

"Something to take your mind off the dream."

Lark sighed, closing her eyes and resting her forehead against him again. She didn't need to ask why — his voice spoke of untold nightmares of his own. "What helps you?"

The wind whistled for the span of a few breaths as Jasper continued to snore, and then Charles answered, his quiet voice soothing. "The laughter of those I adore."

Her mind immediately drifted to a wildflower-filled meadow and she smiled. "That's a pleasant thought."

No more needed to be said, and calmed by his steady heartbeat, the howling of the wind was forgotten. She was muscle and bone, sinew and skin. The warmth from his blood continued to bond with hers, enveloping her, and as Jasper shifted and traded his snores for heavy breaths, she was lulled into a peaceful sleep.

V.

The mountain range was behind them and the open range was before. They had already ridden through the plains for days and yet Lark could see no end to the sea of grass that hissed and sighed with the ebb and flow of the hot prairie breath, like the tide. Small rodents, like bold gophers, peeked out of mounds and stared at their motley caravan from yards away as the group cut through the greens and yellows of the grass.

Bison lowed in the distance and Charles, riding point, stiffened on his mount, his shoulders like the arms of a cross or the ears of a deer. Once she caught sight of a buffalo bull eyeing the horses and riders cutting through his herd, Lark knew why. She couldn't much think of anything uglier or more powerful. The bull's dark eyes and nose glistened in the summer heat, pinpricks of moisture amidst a hulking mountain of brown curling fur and muscle. Their mule wheezed out a screeching greeting, earning a grunt and a cloven hoof pawing at the turf in return.

"Easy there, little fella," Jasper cooed to the bull. "Go along now."

Lark expected their scout to relax once the herd was well in their wake, but he continued to ride like a grizzly on its hind legs — all attention was focused outwards, ever scouring the horizon that kept slipping farther and farther into the setting sun.

When at last they stopped for the evening, Steven and Frank set about stomping down enough grass to make room for bedrolls and a cookfire while Lark and Jasper readied their messware, swatting at mosquitoes kicked up by the blacksmiths. Charles sought high ground, of which there was scant little, and perched himself on a low hill where he could survey the ululating grass that surrounded them. Lark was about to call out to him to tease that the bison weren't exactly following their scent, when she realized the real reason for their scout's disquiet: they had entered Sioux territory.

The salt pork and hard tack were quickly growing unpalatable, so none of the other males took much notice of Charles ignoring them when they called him to eat. Lark did, however. Just as she noticed the dullness of her mind and body when he didn't look at her, for he didn't spare her a glance all evening. As if he expected flames to burst forth in the grass, or his mother to holler for him from the distant reaches of the prairie.

"Will you look at that?" Steven whispered.

Jasper let out a low whistle. Lark watched the sunset with the men, begging for her bones to be shifted by the oranges and pinks arching over her brighter and fuller than she'd ever seen, but deep down, she knew that nothing would ever move her being as much as the thoughts behind green eyes and the rugged promise that knowing all of them would be like trying to reach that horizon.

The night was warmer than any other on the grasslands and the crickets were even louder than Jasper's snores. Lark tossed on her strip of wool and kicked off her boots and stockings, desperate for some measure of coolness or comfort, but there was none. Until a deep voice whispered her name.

"Lark."

She opened her eyes and propped herself up on an elbow, peering around in the dimness of the night, expecting to find Charles at her side. Instead, he was still at his perch several yards off, illuminated by flashes of distant light in the sky. Sitting up, Lark surveyed the other men but they were all asleep. Rising, she stepped carefully, barefoot on the unknown turf. Lights flashed again, highlighting their scout's silhouette, and she used the lightning like a path to the hill.

Charles didn't turn to face her but still spoke. "It won't rain."

"Then what's it from?"

"Heat."

Lark stepped up beside him on the low rise and stared intently at the distance as he did, expecting to glimpse a shape amidst the plains in the next flash of lightning, but the whiteness flickered and fell and she saw nothing but the sea of grass. There were no more forts. No more tent poles of the world she had left behind. Without trees, she had never felt more naked.

"What if we get hit?" she asked.

His hand closed around her wrist with a gentle tug and she nestled down beside him. "We won't. By lightning, anyway," he softly replied.

In the next flash of light, she realized that he had finally given up on the horizon and was gazing upon her face. She hoped he saw in her what she saw in him: tangled manes and long goodnights, spring rains, dried oak leaves and little feet. Lines that led to nowhere but her fingertips. The curve of his cheek and the earth of his voice made her hum more than any song. Charles' gusts stretched and grew the borders of her soul until she understood that, more than anything, the frontier she'd been aching for all her life wasn't a place at all.

She leaned her shoulder against his and he returned the pressure until she felt that they were both being held upright by each other's bodies. When she rested her head on his shoulder, one of his arms encircled her waist as his hand splayed against her ribs, and she thought of the Spanish on the coast and the vastness of the continent and how there must be some corner where no one else ever hunted.

"What's your name?" Lark asked.

"Did you get mule-kicked when I wasn't looking?" he teased.

"Not your Christian name. Your birth name."

Charles sighed and the expanding torso against hers reminded her of a swaying oak trunk though she'd never seen one sway before. "I can't tell you how many times I've tried to recall what my mother called me."

He rested his cheek on the top of her head, his thumb tracing the bumps of her ribs beneath her fabric and skin, and she remembered the stories from her own childhood of how her parents were worried she was a mute when she didn't speak for her first three years and instead imitated birds. The words eventually came, of course. They were just harder to form than the chirps and trills that accompanied her waking hours.

The lights continued their dance overhead, chasing each other from cloud belly to cloud belly as she and Charles watched. He shifted and she felt a hair or two on her scalp twinge as he kissed the top of her head then the crown of her forehead. No more needed to be said, and though she was even warmer pressed against the rushing blood of his body, Lark grew drowsy.

She awoke sometime later as the ground moved beneath her with steady thumps. Carried. Then she was set down onto her wool and as she opened her eyes, she recognized Charles' silhouette outlined by stars. Once he'd settled her down, he leaned back on his haunches to leave so she snared his fingers in hers.

"Stay with me," she whispered, even as Jasper's snoring quieted as his sleep grew shallower.

Charles' voice was hoarse and low. "You know I can't."

She let her hand fall limply to her side and it hit her bedroll with a thud. She could see the scout's shoulders rise and fall with yearning but couldn't tell if she was feeling his exhale or the breeze. Her hair that had escaped her braid was in twisted, sticky knots, and as he brushed them off her cheek she wondered how he could see her in the moonlessness. When he kissed her forehead proper, she closed her eyes, absorbing the prickle of his chin hairs on her nose bridge and the dryness of his lips, even as his body smelled of sharp sweat and moisture in the heat.

He pulled away and she took a moment to weave the scent and feel of him into her heartstrings before opening her eyes. Charles was gone and she was faced instead with a cloudless night. The stars were so numerous and visible in the openness that she couldn't fathom a king needing anything more than the jewels of the sky.

Charles tread quietly back to his perch, kicking up fireflies in his wake that drifted behind him as if they'd fallen from above and traded their silver for gold.

For a moment, before he reached his sentry hill, the scout appeared to have finally melded with the black line of the horizon.

VI.

They were separated seconds after the gunfire erupted as the mounted warriors circled their horses and mule. Charles pushed Lark onto the ground behind a prairie dog mound and Jasper slid down beside her as they sought cover.

"They want the horses," the scout shouted as he dashed into the midst of their white-eyed equines, snatching up their reins. "Don't shoot!"

"Like hell I won't," Frank snapped back, on one knee beside his brother who was hastily reloading his musket.

Lark's eyes were stung with sand as a brave galloped past her, letting out a whoop, and she covered her head and stayed down when she felt her brother's hand against her shoulder blades. Their own horses were stamping and groaning, like a stream that had no choice but to join the river of the other swarming steeds. The turf beneath her body shook with each gallop, screaming at her to do something more than hide. Lark rose to her knees in time to see Steven fire buckshot sky-high. The pounding drum of the attacking hooves grew muffled as the band widened their circle and then surged towards a copse of cottonwood trees lining a river ravine.

"God Almighty," Steven gasped, pivoting to watch the retreat.

With a throaty whine, Lark's mare yanked her reins loose from Charles' hand and bolted after the retreating party.

"That ain't your damn herd," Jasper called after the fleeing horse.

Shoving the rest of the horses' leads into Steven's hands, Charles took off after the mare at a lope as she disappeared into the trees.

"Charles," Frank scolded, but the scout didn't stop.

Lark climbed to her feet, her blouse clinging to the sweat slicking her skin and dripping between her breasts. "Are they gone?" she gasped.

"That was your horse," Jasper clarified.

"Charles?" she called as he disappeared into the cottonwoods.

"Do we go after him?" Steven asked.

"If anyone knows these Brulé bastards, it's Charles."

Maybe it was the casual way her brother said the words, but Lark acted without a second thought. Snatching the musket out of Jasper's hands, she broke into a sprint, following the torn up earth left behind by so many hooves.

"Lark," Jasper snarled, chasing after her, but she had always been faster and didn't look back. Not even when she heard him stop.

The blood that rushed past her ears pulsed like a drum, muffling all other noise as she neared the ravine and the trees. Scrambling down the hillside, her boots splashed into the warm water of the creek her party had been trying to reach before they were surrounded. The hillside was sandy and covered in dead leaves and leftover tufts of cottony seeds from the spring. She fell forward once as she scaled the other bank and nearly pulled the trigger, but kept going as if she couldn't stop. Once on the other side of the ravine, the trees were thicker and so was the sand, as if the sunbaked region had once flooded.

Jasper shouted in the distance but she ignored what was behind. While she expected a trail of torn up earth or a mass of painted shapes retreating into the distance, the only indication she had of where the band had fled was the backside of her own mare, distorted by heat waves, galloping in pursuit of the other horses, useless stirrups flapping at her sides.

"Charles?" she panted, wiping the sweat off her trigger hand and surveying the grove around her as she raised her voice. "Charles?"

There was no answer. Pressing her lips together, she fought to quiet her breathing enough to hear more than just her body. The breeze stuck her tangled strands to her sticky skin, rattling the spade-shaped leaves until the trees around her became a chorus of laughing ghosts. The birds that chattered in their branches sounded foreign and sharp.

Apprehension made her voice shrill. "Charles?"

The wind shifted and she held her breath, eyes wide. Her name had been in that gust before it was taken over by the gossiping cottonwoods. Still as a rabbit, she strained her ears. The wind died and she heard it again, coming from the west. It was Charles's voice. Armed as she was, Lark dashed towards her name. After a few heartbeats she slowed, waiting for a guiding response. When there was none, she drew a breath to call his name again. Before she could let it out, she heard a branch break to her left and ran in that direction, musket at the ready.

Yet no manner of weaponry or readiness could have protected her from what she found.

Charles tried to step away from a trunk, stumbling to his knees. The lower half of his shirt was soaked with dark blood. She gasped then had to fight off the urge to turn away, instead slowly lowering her firearm as she studied his face. He was peering down at his hands resting on his stomach around a protruding knife hilt. When his body spasmed, he pulled them away and sluggishly turned them over, palms up, the dark liquid glinting in the sunlight. His gaze found Lark and the betrayed fear in his eyes constricted her throat.

She stumbled forward and tossed the musket aside, noting how the blood also coated his buckskins but reminding herself that spilled milk always looked like more than it was.

"Lark..." His voice was a cracked, pleading gasp that made her heart miss a beat. He seemed dizzy and looked down, disoriented, before toppling over backwards with a choked grunt.

Falling to her knees beside him, she grabbed his shoulders and eased him into her lap. "I'm right here, Charles."

He awkwardly straightened his legs and she had never seen his skin come so close to matching hers.

"Jasper," she screamed. "Jasper!"

A reply came but whatever words it contained were drowned out by the hiss and rattle of the leaves overhead. Their quivering shadows dappled the scout's body, shifting shade around the knife hilt and another dark tear in his tunic, marking a second wound.

Charles' muscles were tight and he whined and dug his heels into the sand, pushing it about into little piles as he shook. Lark tugged on her sleeves, shrugging off her blouse, the memory of the first time she'd held him flickering behind her eyes as firelight dancing off cave walls. She leaned over him and pressed her wadded fabric to the open wound on his flank as her own stench blended with the iron of blood. Too much blood. It was stealing her breath.

He gritted his teeth, beads of sweat adorning his temple as he grunted out speech. "Traitor. They think I'm a traitor."

She nodded, resting a hand on his cheek, her brows furrowed at the effort his speaking required. "They're gone. They've left."

The scout squeezed his eyes shut and the sunlight shimmered on a teardrop in the corner of one. He let out his breath in a roared gasp, his body shuddering.

"Take it out." His right hand resting on his stomach clenched and clawed the air near the knife hilt.

Lark was no doctor, but knew from trapping and hunting that to do so would only open the wound further. She tried to reply that she couldn't, but the words were too difficult to form as her tongue swelled up in her brain the longer she stared at the antler hilt of the knife. Knife. In him.

She couldn't tell if it was his pain or hers surging through their touching skin, searing her edges. She couldn't blink. She couldn't smell. She wasn't a person anymore. Just a body.

Boots splashed in the creek below and a man panted as he climbed the sandy embankment. "Jesus Christ — what the hell happened?"

"I found him," Lark told her brother, but her voice felt like it came from underwater as Charles' back hardened against her thighs.

"Jasper," the scout wheezed. "Out. Pull it out." Tears slipped out of his eyes and down his temples, darkening twin patches of Lark's trousers. "Please."

She had never heard him sound like that before and for a moment, tried to convince herself that he was actually someone else, and that she had been mistaken all along. That his jade eyes, reddened with tears and pain, weren't the same that she awoke every morning to see. That she hunted for like a baying hound.

Jasper stared at something a yard away in the grass. It was straight and had feathers. An arrow, or what was left of one. Her brother inspected the wound it had made in his friend's flank then set his jaw as he did every time he had to remove the iron teeth of a trap off of a kill as a youth. "Hold his shoulders," he said quietly.

Lark felt a little more of her lines fade. "Jasper —"

"It don't make a difference now," he lowly hissed as Charles groaned and repetitively scraped a heel against the sand.

"You're stronger. I'll do it." Her vocal chords formed the words and she moved without knowing she could.

Then she was kneeling beside the scout's hips as Jasper leaned down against the larger man's shoulders. Her fingers wrapped around the pale antler of the hilt and sweat stung her eyes.

"On the count of three," Jasper said.

Charles's left hand dug into the sand while his right gripped Jasper's forearm as he attempted to brace himself for what was to come.

Lark took a few shallow breaths to fight off the heat burning the boundaries of her being, but all it did was feed the fire. "One... Two..."

Something in her chest revolted against the word three, reminding her that she wasn't formless, after all. That she could still have minutes, even if they were selfish.

"Three."

In one fluid movement, Lark leaned forward, pressing down on the scout's stomach with her left hand and pulling the knife out.

Charles screamed, the sound cringing her hot edges until having a body or not didn't matter anymore because for the moment, she still existed and so did he. He went limp and breathed in whimpers as blood gushed from the new opening. Jasper grabbed his sister's blouse and pressed it against the flow, but she had seen enough blackened red for one lifetime, and instead scooted to Charles' other end. His eyes were half lidded with exhaustion as the brown of his skin faded into numbness while his life fled peacefully.

The leaves of the cottonwoods rattled, loosening some of their stray down into the air. It floated past the trio in lackadaisical tufts. She had been that drifting white.

When cold fingers brushed against the back of her hand, she knew without a doubt that she was anchored to this moment like the pin in the center of a compass that was always searching for a fifth direction. Charles' fingers left red stripes on the back of her hand and she sought his face. His green eyes were tilted up at hers and the marring pain was gone. She could see Charles again, and that made her smile. When he smiled back she knew that she wasn't nothingness at all and never had been. She was everything.

"Father in heaven," Jasper whispered, rocking back and forth as he pressed against the wound, his eyes closed, "Hallowed be your name…"

A soft whimper escaped the scout and she couldn't tell if it was from pain or trying to speak.

Jasper lifted the stained blouse to look beneath, his voice mildly hopeful. "The bleeding's slowing."

Like her brother, Lark pretended that it wasn't because there was only so much blood in a body. She laid her hand against Charles' jawbone, hoping to still the spinning of his compass needle, but his eyes were glassy, and she knew he no longer saw the world as she and Jasper did. Maybe he never had. "I'm here."

His voice was barely above a whisper and blended with the breeze. "So am I."

Lark smiled.

The trees surrounding the glade rustled quietly, filling the moment of defeated human silence until a long hissing breath eased out of the scout and faded into the rattling of the spinning leaves.

Jasper cursed, leaning back on his haunches, and hurled the wadded up blouse away from him. Lark watched as a film spread over Charles' eyes, and once he looked like the stranger she had first met when he'd asked to share their fire after crossing the Ohio, she pulled her hand away from his face and howled. Because she was both a woman and the wind. Jasper pulled her away, wrapping his body around her as if he could shield the weeping wound that was growing inside, but she knew her brother's cradling arms could never again be enough to comfort her.

VII.

Lark had ignored Jasper's gentle cautioning and cleaned the body alone. Her face was stony as she wiped at the crusting red. She hadn't even taken the time to change out of her dark-stained camisole, as if Charles' blood linked her to him.

The voices of the others several yards off by the horses carried to her on the breeze every now and then. Jasper was relating what had happened to the brothers and discussing where to lay the body to rest. Lugging the large man's corpse across the stream and back to the blacksmiths was easier than it had any right to have been. Either because the scout had been emptied of so much blood, or because without him breathing, Lark kept slipping in and out of herself.

She clenched her jaw, dipping her cloth in the rusty water of their pot again and glancing at the flies fighting over Charles's mouth and eyes before wiping at his abdomen once more, irritated that someone like Steven Smith, who once tried to be a banker and could barely understand Charles and the circumstances that made him who he was, would have any input on where he would wish to be buried. When his words "what about just high-tailing it..." carried to her, Lark shot the males a glower. They could run all they liked, but she would bury Charles.

Her already-chilled insides gave a small writhe and she looked back at his stomach, realizing with some measure of surprise that she'd finished. But she didn't want to be finished. Not with him.

Resting her hand on his hipbone, she studied his face. Other than the flies that she had given up battling, he still looked so alive that she focused on him, willing his eyes to open and his chest to rise, the task seeming so insanely simple. Breathe, just breathe. That's all anyone had to do to live. But Charles' chest didn't move, and with a gasp, Lark filled her lungs with much-needed air. She hadn't even realized that she'd been holding her breath. Or maybe she'd been holding it ever since she crossed the Ohio and was just now exhaling.

A young man and a young woman should never cohabit a space alone. They might find something they enjoy in the way the other laughs or moves through the world. In the way fireflies chase buckskins and the way a man and a mountain can be so lithic that there's no telling where one begins and the other ends.

She pressed her fingertips to Charles' temple, tracing the wide arch of his cheekbone, realizing that a band of freckles was just starting to bloom across the bridge of his nose but never had the time to darken enough for her to notice. Because she was never usually this close to his lips in the broad daylight.

A throat cleared behind her.

"At last," she croaked. "My chaperone."

Jasper crouched beside her and though she tried not to, she noticed that the slimy gelatin that had become Charles' eyes didn't move to acknowledge her brother.

"You know it wasn't ever like that."

"No. I don't think you could keep track of me if you tried."

"I wouldn't try."

Lark was surprised by the stiffness of her body as she twisted to face her brother. Jasper held his hat in one hand and was peering down at Charles.

"Almost seems like he's sleeping."

"Almost."

Jasper waved his hat over the body, kicking up a cloud of flies. He waited a moment before speaking again. "We were just discussing —"

"I heard."

"Steven wants to give him a Christian burial."

The Fuhrmanns used to read to them from the Bible Sunday nights. It was the only time the other children would sit on the ground with Lark and Jasper. Their hair was so yellow, their skin so pink.

"But I think I've got him convinced to leave the choice up to you," Jasper continued. "After all... you knew him best."

She knew the boughs of the oak and the stoic stance of the grizzly. The tickle of butterfly legs and the brush of a storm, but now she was just a needle without a compass.

"I don't know what Crow burial rites are, but... I figure he'd be happy with whatever you chose for him."

"There is no North," she whispered.

Jasper rested his hand on her shoulder and gave it a firm squeeze.

In the days that followed, Lark rode Charles' horse and couldn't tell if the intensity of the sun sharpened or dulled her senses. The endlessness of grass stretched on before them and the blacksmiths whispered that Charles' silence had passed on to her. That God worked in mysterious ways and that there wasn't a place for a woman who thought she was a man, and an Indian who thought he was white, anyway. They worried that the browned bloodstains on her camisole would attract predators in the night but she refused to take it off.

One evening, after they had at long last glimpsed something dark on the horizon interrupting the prairie, like a canyon, Jasper pulled Lark into a hug.

"It ain't right," he cooed as held her. "It ain't right."

Then Lark felt his hands tugging at her clothing and tried to escape but his arms were firm. She yowled and clawed.

"Damnit, Lark, I don't mean you any harm!"

She stomped on his toes with the heel of her boot just as she had dozens of times in their youth then tore off when he released her. Mosquitoes whined as they hunted her heat, kicked up by her passing, but Lark didn't slow. She ran until her lungs were aching but no matter how far she went, she could still see their camp on the emptiness of the plains. Could still feel their eyes. Their judgment.

As much as she wanted to blame Charles for awakening this restlessness in her, she knew it was a lie. It had always been there. The jade eyes of her shoulder-companion had brought spring to her soul, but now his bones were scattered across the prairie and in the bellies of coyotes, and the wilderness inside her was cavernous and hungry for something she couldn't have.

"I'm right here," she whispered through her tears. "Where are you?"

By the time she realized that she didn't want to know the answer, the sun had set and the crickets in the thick grass around her were chirping so loudly that there was no end or beginning to the sound. Just a cacophony of courtship.

Then a breeze kicked up a cluster of fireflies as they abandoned their swaying strands of grass and she heard it for the first time since Charles' death. It was as if the very dirt throbbed beneath her feet and the air around her hummed. The windsong was just as much a part of the landscape as the rocks and trees and yet she had rarely ever quieted enough to actually listen until

Charles. Listen. Because the whispers of life were everywhere and weren't really whispers at all. They were as bold and yearning as the fern reaching for the sun and the buffalo bull throwing his heavy horned head.

Lark smiled, for there was a difference between walking on the sod and walking with it, just as enduring the seasons was separate from moving as a part of them. Her entire being thrummed with a pulse that lay much deeper than the rock shelf below the soil, and was much older than any thought.

A wolf wailed from far too close and yet not close enough. The vibrating canine chords shook the hollowed place inside where she understood that she would never wake up and see jade eyes again. When the lone bay was joined by others, forming a chorus, she knew the men at the camp behind her would be frightened for themselves and the woman who had wandered into the midst of wolves. The thought made Lark laugh, but she couldn't hear her own sound as one yowl blended into another until all else faded and there was only the howling and the beckoning of the mountains so very far away.

Epilogue

Lark struck out on her own about a year after Charles's death. It wasn't anything dramatic, it was just her time to head out. And truth be told, she wasn't ever the same after he died.

We bid farewell to the Smith brothers by the coast then headed north to a range the Spanish called the snow-covered saw, or Sierra Nevada. There were plenty of times we never thought we'd make it to California, but I reckon we only did because our party was so small as to not be a bother to much anyone who lived in the land we passed through. I'd say that having fewer people to share our resources with was also an aid but not with the way Frank and Steven ate.

My sister lived in an abandoned cabin I'd helped her fix up a few miles outside of town, on the edge of my land up in the foothills. The Spanish have a taste for beef, and I found work as a drover before long. She earned a living fur trapping and the poor thing was a joke among most of the women in town on account of her uncombed hair and trousers. We grew apart. Neither of us intended for it to happen, but what with auctions and drives, I wasn't in one spot nearly as much as I ought to have been.

About three years down the line, I came home from a cattle drive in late summer only to learn that she was engaged to some feller I hadn't ever heard of. Naturally, I went to see her, even if I couldn't decide if I wanted to give the lucky fella a good kick in the trousers or a clap on the back.

Her house was practical and uncluttered, almost bare, and she let in only enough light so that we could function. But that wasn't the queer part. The queer part was seeing my sister, Lark Ferguson, in a God damn dress. I couldn't be sure, but she may have even been wearing a corset. The cabin suddenly felt like a cage.

Lark smiled as she handed me a cup of coffee and asked how I was. Her hair was combed and fell on her shoulders in curling clumps which I'd never much seen before since she was accustomed to a braid ever since we were small.

"There's good money in cattle," I replied as I showed off my tailored suit.

She smiled at that, but I could tell it was forced. She could never much tell the difference between something fine and something commonplace, anyway. It may have been a dress on her body but it wasn't a frilly one.

"So what's this I hear about you being engaged?"

Lark glanced away towards the window, as if I'd brought up something frivolous, then seemed to realize her reaction and fixed me with another forced smile. "James."

I nodded, not really knowing what to say. I'd forgotten how she had a tendency to trail off every now and then, as if being alone for so long had made her forget that most people find pleasure in conversing. "He's got a nice name, I'll give him that much." I narrowed my eyes at her, trying to tease out the sister I'd grown up with catching fish. "He's got excellent taste, too."

The smile was real this time, and in the dim light I thought I saw her cheeks color a little. I shut up, waiting for her to speak further. To find out more about my future brother-in-law.

Instead, she rose and ladled us some stew. I thanked her and we ate in silence for a few minutes before the quiet got to me and I couldn't help but smirk in memory of many similar moments I'd spent with Charles. The quiet never seemed to bother him, and my attempts at conversation were often met with the briefest answers possible.

"Lark, I trust you to make this decision on your own, but what kind of man is he? Have you two set a date yet? And how the hell can you cure a hide in that thing?" I gestured to her long skirt.

Her gaze had fixed on the door behind me but her eyes were unfocused. Once she took a deep breath and exhaled before her brown eyes met mine, I knew I'd stepped into something sticky. "James is... a very kind man."

It was eerie. She fed me that practiced line with practiced happiness.

"He doesn't much mind my independence. I'm very fortunate to have him."

I set my spoon aside. "But...?"

She shrugged, leaning back in her chair, looking out the window at the falling leaves, but I could tell by the way her face was turned that her gaze was on the distant mountains. When she returned her attention to me, something had shifted in her eyes, and she seemed older and feverish at the same time. She'd shed her mask and now looked upon me as the brother I was, her voice deepening into a confiding tone. "Try as I might, Jasper, I... I can't set a date. Not even a season."

"Has he been pressuring you to?"

Lark shook her head immediately, wrapping her hands around her cup of coffee. "No, but we've been courting for almost a year. Most women wed within the first few months of engagement. Or so I hear."

I nodded, even if only to hide the fact that I was regretting the time I'd spent away. She didn't seem to ever begrudge me for it. She didn't seem to ever begrudge me for anything. "Do you love him?"

Her eyes latched onto mine and the fever-heat in their brown orbs only grew hotter. "He's a trapper."

"That ain't an answer."

"He has a bad leg and no one else will want him."

"Lark?"

She looked out the window to the mountains again, her hands still cupping her mug, as if it was the only thing grounding her in time. A gust of wind fluttered the curtains, rattling the vase of dried wildflowers on the windowsill. "It's just that..." she trailed off, her eyes glassy.

"He's not Charles," I finished for her.

That was all it took. When she focused on me again the feverishness was gone and she was the same young thing I'd taken West with me. Or maybe it was her who'd taken me. Either way, I'd taken a risk by mentioning the half-breed, but the chiseled truth in her gaze told me that I'd never been more right. The wind tossed a bit of her hair over her shoulder and she glanced down to where the lock came to rest against her left breast, above her heart. Her answer was quiet, almost whispered. "No... he ain't."

"Yeah." I sighed. "I miss him, too."

Lark's eyes first lingered on the wildflowers on the sill then gazed at the Sierras out the window, as if she could hear their voices.

I knew she missed him more than I did — more than I ever could. He wasn't just our scout or even our friend to her. They had a bond I always struggled to understand, and always failed to. But I knew from the moment she looked at me, helpless and lost as he lay dying, that she loved him. And I know now that he would forever be to her what a dream is to the dreamer. She would always wonder what could have been, and she would always treasure what they had together.

The wind was at his back now, wherever he may be, roaming the ranges and haunting the hills, untamed, free. He'd forever be a ghost on her breath. He'd forever be the cry of the wolf, haunting the wilderness of the land and the heart alike. He'd forever be her wild frontier.

A tear slipped out of the corner of her eye, disappearing into the shadows of the dim light.

I sighed, wishing I had the grace with words that our mother did, and the wisdom to go with it. "I can't tell you what to do, Lark."

She wiped at her cheekbone when another tear escaped.

"But I know he'd want you to be happy... whatever you decide."

I rose and crossed to her and she stood, falling into my arms with a hushed sob and a whispered, "I know."

As I held her, I realized that I was probably the only one who could ever understand, for I was the only one who ever knew the both of them well enough to have glimpsed what they'd shared, even if only in the light in Lark's eyes when she spoke of him.

I didn't offer her any more advice, for I had no more to give, aside from a firm beating if ever this James deserved it. The choice was hers and hers alone. As I left, I promised that I'd always be here if she needed to talk, and she gave me a grateful smile and a thank-you.

I don't know if what I said helped or hindered her, but not a week later, she staked her dress to the front door, like a farewell, and disappeared. The last time I saw her was as I began to close her door that late summer day as the sun set. She stood still as a statue, a gust of wind playing with her hair, her gaze on the beckoning wilds, just out of reach.

About the Author

K.M. RICE is a national award-winning writer who has worked for both Magic Leap and Weta Workshop, the latter being responsible for such cinematic epics as *The Lord of the Rings* and *The Hobbit*.

Her first novel, *Darkling*, is a young adult fantastical thriller. When not working on her novels or hiking in the woods, she can be found enjoying the company of the many animals on her family ranch in the Santa Cruz Mountains.

Several years in the making, her upcoming Afterworld series is set to debut with the first book, *Ophelia*.

Made in the USA
Middletown, DE
31 May 2015